ELLIOT STANTON

Can It Be Just Me?

Poetic Observations On Modern Life

This book is dedicated to all those who "get me".

Contents

ANOTHER YEAR, SAME OLD EXCUSE

There are those of us who enjoy and embrace it,
There are those of us who it fills with fear.
Whether we like to party or ignore it completely,
All In the name of welcoming in the New Year.

'What are you planning for New Year's Eve?'
Is the question so many of us dread.
'Oh, nothing much. I'm just having a quiet one.'
Meaning, 'By 10 pm, I'll probably be in bed.'

'We're having a do at our place. Come along.'
A kind gesture, but not one I care to receive.
'I'll just check with the wife and let you know,'
You say, desperately searching for excuses to deceive.

Don't get me wrong; I've had some great New Year's Eves,
Especially the ones spent with friends in my youth.
Full of laughs, great company and crazy antics,
Featuring bawdy behaviour and generally being uncouth.

In later years, if I'd decided to go out,
I'd prefer a more sedate and placid affair.
With just a few friends, several drinks and nice food,
And not out too late as I'd arranged childcare.

And woe betide me if I'd already committed,
To put on a little party at my place.
Is there enough food for everyone who I invited?
And what if there's just not enough space?

To the present day, I now like to stay indoors,
Let others bring in the New Year with a blast.
I'm happy enough to view the celebrations on TV,
Not at all feeling like a social outcast...

I might sound like a right old miserable git,
But it's how I like to spend that particular night.
Revelry and debauchery might still suit some of my age,
But 'just having a quiet one' is my personal highlight.

* * *

HOLE IN THE GROUND

"Roadworks here, until the end of June",
Was the quote on the muddy, yellow sign,
Besides a hole that's become so familiar,
It's almost developed into a local shrine.

A solitary workman is seen now and again,
Digging out a shovel or two of earth,
Before disappearing on a well-deserved break,
Perhaps, to re-evaluate his worth.

Over eight weeks into the same task,
It's hard to see what has been done.
Apart from upsetting the flow of traffic,
And to detour folk out on their morning run.

Orange cones topped with flashing lamps,
Alert passers-by to the ongoing 'work'.
Around the usually empty and dirty landmark,
Which is driving the poor locals berserk.

A few weeks ago, there was a flurry of activity-
A delivery of yellow pipes were made.
They were left by the hole overnight,
And by daybreak, they had mysteriously strayed.

The hole is usually filled with beer cans,
Following the weekend, on a Monday.
Along with bottles, cigarette butts and other detritus,
The workman's first job is to clear them away.

Last Friday morning, I walked to the shops,
But paused to sit on a nearby bench.
I observed the hard-hatted, hi-vised, young man,
Digging his hole, which was becoming a trench.

The youthful lad, seemingly proud of his effort,
Paused his repetitive task, to light up a fag.
He leant on his shovel and soaked up the sun,
And wiped his sweaty brow on a dirty rag.

Twenty minutes later, and on my return,
The hole was unattended once more.
Perhaps the lad had taken an early lunch,
And would be back at his post by half-four.

Today, however– an exciting development,
Another hard-hatted, hi-vised lad came by.
He dropped off a new sign to side of the hole-
"Roadworks here, until the end of July".

* * *

4

SILLY AISLES

Just when I'd got used to the old layout,
The manager of my supermarket had a brainwave.
To re-arrange everything that I usually shop for.
He really needs to stop meddling and behave.

Fresh fruit is where the vegetables once were,
And dairy produce has replaced cooked meat.
I knew exactly where to go for my breakfast cereal,
Now heaven knows what's happened to my Shredded Wheat.

I had a routine; a set method, if you will,
I knew exactly what aisles to walk down and why.
But now furniture polish and Hoover bags reside,
Where once I found my steak and ale pie.

Greetings cards, magazines and books have been replaced,
By baby clothes and other such paraphernalia.
And the fruit juice, yoghurt and trifles have been swapped,
With bacon and cooked ham from Westfalia.

Sauces, relishes, sliced beetroot and pickles,
Are now located opposite shelves of tinned fruit.
And where one used to find packets of pasta,
There's Beef Wellington and salmon en croûte.

Washing up liquid, bleach and limescale remover,
Are now stacked neatly in aisle seventeen.
That's where I used to find ready-cooked Asian food,
Such as chicken madras and beef in black bean.

If it ain't broke, don't fix it, my Dad used to say.
I think that changing the store layout is plain silly.
I don't need to be confronted with boxes of cat food,
When all I want is a small jar of piccalilli.

The bakery, thank goodness, is still in the same place,
Although I've not seen a baguette or French stick in ages.
Perhaps the plan is to remove it altogether,
With bread products simply disappearing in stages.

Maybe I'm getting conservative in my old age,
But I do like to know where I can find things.
If I'm looking for a block of parmesan cheese,
I don't want to be confronted by chicken wings.

Why couldn't they have left things as they were?
I watch a shoplifter get confused before he legs it.
He panics as he tries to make his escape,
Because the old entrance is now the new exit.

* * *

CRAP IN THE ATTIC

It shouldn't be dramatic to enter your attic,
To search for a box of old photos.
But as I turned on the light, I got such a fright,
By the amount of crap in the shadows.

A sack full of toys for two-year-old boys,
Was the first thing I happened to see.
A wooden train track; building blocks to stack,
And a teddy bear with a bandaged knee.

The next thing I saw was a half-broken drawer,
Inside it, a Dorchester Hotel ashtray.
The reason it was there, I wasn't aware,
But maybe it will be valuable one day.

And gathering dust was a miniature bust,
Of King Henry VIII in stern royal pose.
Bought on a school trip to see his warship,
In Portsmouth, the Mary Rose.

Curtains and drapes; knick-knacks of all shapes,
Lay atop a decrepit French dresser.
Along with a heap of hubcaps, stainless steel bath taps,
And a broken Braun food processor.

Water bowls for pets, cutlery sets,
And a large ceramic Great Dane,
Should have been chucked, so that they couldn't obstruct,
My traipse through the treacherous terrain.

And on the far wall was a paddling pool,
How the hell did it get over there?
Along with a lamp and a strong smell of damp,
Was an unassembled flat-pack bath chair.

Heaters and fans; pots and pans,
In neat piles, lay on the floor.
And up against the gable, a dining-room table,
And half of my old kitchen door.

After an hour of searching and perilous perching,
I sadly realised the photos weren't there.
So somewhat downbeat, I conceded defeat,
And departed the loft in despair.

One day I'll scrap that load of old crap,
A promise I'll keep, I swear.
So, I turned off the light and closed the hatch tight,
To look for the photos elsewhere.

* * *

THE FAKEST FAKE

There are fakes, and there is what I'm looking at today.
The worst I've ever seen; I totally dismay.
Would a Rolex by any other name tick so sweet?
Well, it certainly doesn't look or feel complete.

A gentleman, if I am generous, wants to sell his watch,
But what he hands me barely reaches bottom notch.
A wonky face and a missing digit alert me to check,
The timepiece equivalent of a terrible train wreck.

'It's an unwanted gift,' the gentleman gladly tells me.
Of course, it is. Why would he want to keep this monstrosity?
The plating is peeling; the bracelet is badly bent.
I've seen many a knock-off Rolex, but never to this extent.

I weigh it up in my hand, which gives me a huge clue,
To the validity of the watch, which is supposed to be "almost new".
Even a Mickey Mouse Timex is a weightier piece,
And be costlier than this crap that was created to fleece.

The time on a broken watch will be correct twice a day,
But the hour hand is bent, trapped on the date display.
For fun, I shake it to start the automatic wind,
Something sounds loose-unless it's the way it's designed.

I could go on about the rough edges and faded crown,
But I grow weary, so I gently let the customer down.
I'm afraid to say, sir, this watch isn't real.
'Oh, I'm sure is,' he replies, making a half-hearted appeal.

Being subtle and calm is clearly not going to work,
I need to be more straightforward to this ignorant berk.
'It's a fake. A bad one. The worst I've ever seen.
It's not worth a fiver, a pound. Not a single bean.'

He gazes at me in silence, then at the watch,
For a moment, heartbroken, in need of a wee nip of Scotch.
Then he slowly cups it into his quivering hand.
'Fair enough, guv. I'll bin it as originally planned.'

* * *

PIZZA THE ACTION

The delivery usually takes just twenty minutes,
From ordering to arriving at the front door.
But it's the pre-show that gets me so frustrated-
The regular 'toppings argument' I so abhor.

'I've gone off the meat feast; there's too much... meat.'
'Last time, the mozzarella was like elastic.'
'The sweetcorn had dried out in the oven,
It was like biting on little pieces of plastic.'

'Make up your mind on what you want, kids.
How about an extra-large chicken supreme?'
Apparently, the chicken's too dry, and peppers are "yuk".
So, overall the pizza is somewhat less than 'reem'.

And then there's the base, another endless debate,
Do you want thin and crispy or deep pan?
Of course, no consensus can be immediately agreed.
We're as far away on a decision as when we began.

'Tell you what, your mother and I will have the Hawaiian.
And yes, I'll scrape the pineapple off your half, dear.
And you kids can have a large plain Margarita -
That's tomato and cheese, so there's nothing to fear.'

Finally, we are settled on our choices,
And the call to the pizza place could be made.
'Sorry folks, they no longer deliver here,' I sighed
'Who fancies McDonald's?' I waited, and I prayed.

* * *

TEASE UP!

Hurry up and drink your tea before it goes cold.
- I'll have it soon. It's a bit too hot right now.
But what's the point of a mug of freezing cold tea?
-I'll drink it when my tongue and lips will allow.

You won't feel the benefit if it's not boiling hot.
- My mouth won't benefit third-degree burns.
Stop being such a big drama queen, you silly fool.
- You mean like you when you're having "one of your turns"?

You know - you can make your own tea next time.
- Did I ask you to get up and make me a mug?
No, but I'm considerate, unlike you, you ungrateful git.
- Like I was when I changed your hairdryer plug?

I need to wash up, so drink it now or forget it.
-I've forgotten it, so you might as well take it away.
I don't know why I bothered to even fill up the kettle.
-Oh great, my wife, the martyr's having a field day.

Why did you say you wanted one when you didn't?

- I suppose I didn't want to disappoint you, my dear.

You did that 30 years ago, the day you said "yes".

- Why we even got married is somewhat unclear.

Look, why are we arguing over a stupid mug of tea?

- I don't know. I'm sorry for behaving like a twit.

Me too. Finish your tea, and I'll wash up your mug.

- Hellfire, woman, you just don't know when to quit!

* * *

VAR

'What was VAR, Dad, and why was it banned?'
'Because, son, it ruined the game, you must understand.'
'But wasn't it used to uphold laws and rules?'
'It did, but it also made the refs look like complete fools.'

'I heard that it prevented play-acting and cheating?'
'That it did, son, but folks kept on bleating.
In far away Stockley Park, decisions were made,
Relayed back to the refs; the fans left dismayed.'

The powers that be said the quarrels would end,
But in reality, the game never needed to mend.
The eternal wait for an offside decision then stole,
The player's unbridled joy of scoring a goal.

'But what for handballs? Surely, VAR worked like a charm?'
Well, my boy, that was all about the position of the arm.
Something to do with the "natural silhouette,"
Caused no end of controversy and left folks upset.

Lines on the pitch and monitors at the side,
Superfluous technology we began to deride.
For pundits and fans, confusion did peak,
More disputes and problems, week after week.

'Penalty! Offside!' Fans used to shout.
Then all of a sudden, 'V...A...R!!' widely rang out.
The enjoyment of the game began to wane,
The people got angry; the FA was under strain.

Something had to be done by the powers above,
To save the beautiful game that all of us love.
'Let the onfield ref make decisions,' we cried,
And implement the rules that need to be applied.

So VAR was ended without even a hitch,
Ultimately replaced with four refs on the pitch.
Each one argues and tells the others they're wrong.
And that is why matches are now three hours long.

* * *

THE CUSTOMER IS ALWAYS WRONG

The biggest single myth in retail, I was told,
Is that the customer is always right.
When in actual fact the opposite is true,
And I'm not trying to sound trite.

There are several pieces missing.
–They're all there and complete in the kit.
It was bought for me as a birthday gift.
–No, I served you myself when you paid for it.

As a shopkeeper, you know your stock,
How things work and their actual cost.
So when a chancer questions your retail knowledge,
He's inevitably always wrong. His argument lost.

I bought it here just two weeks ago.
–Your receipt says it was late last year.
It was like that when I purchased it. Honest.
–No, it was new, without a scratch or a smear.

Treat the punter with extreme suspicion.
It's their job in life to cheat and deceive.
But appear sympathetic and listen intently,
And always keep an answer up your sleeve.

You said I could have my money back.
–I said I would replace it for you.
You told me it had a 12-month guarantee.
–But it's a three-pack of economy super glue!

'The trick,' he said, 'is to let them *think* they're right.'
Even though that's rarely ever true.
A smile and a calm voice will enhance the illusion,
That you value the opinion that they've come to.

You said it came with free batteries.
–It's mains powered; it's a bloody kettle!
How do I know the toaster won't melt?
–Don't worry about that, madam; it's made of metal.

After working with the public at large,
For a large chunk of my working life,
I'm not sure that this advice is completely accurate.
They're not all out to cause you strife.

This advice was offered in all sincerity,
By someone who has been wronged many times.
He'd become embittered by the public at large,
And their numerous and most heinous crimes.

* * *

TEST CRICKET IS BORING

'Test match cricket is boring. Nothing ever happens,'
Cry the uninitiated, showing no apparent taste.
The game is played in the mind as much as on the field,
And has to be thought out, planned and paced.

While some versions are played in coloured clothes,
With a white ball under stark floodlights,
The real spectacle is the four-innings test match,
Not in blue pyjamas, but original cricket whites.

The traditional five-day test is just that,
The bowler has to *think* the batsman out.
Adding patience and agility to their skill set,
Along with physical strength and a certain amount of clout.

It's very tough, almost impossible to explain,
To those who view the sport as a joke,
Why you're in when you're out, and out when you're in,
And that a player can even nip off for a smoke.

Cricket is a game packed full of innuendos,
Whilst wearing your V-necked knitted sweater,
You can caress one through the covers if you like,
But stroking your ball down to long leg is far better.

For player and spectator, there's nothing quite like it–
During what other sport do you stop to eat two meals?
And have a 90-minute kip while the action takes place,
Only woken by the bowler's loud appeals?

I'm not going to get all technical and preachy,
And go into the subtle intricacies of the game.
But if you happen to like statistics and years of tradition,
Then cricket will certainly light your flame.

So, in closing, I doubt I could ever convince,
Those who haven't taken the game to their heart.
But if eating and sleeping is what you want from your sport.
Then Test cricket is worth a watch if you're smart.

* * *

WINDOWS UPDATE

There's a Windows Update I'd been putting off for a while,
For over two weeks, if the truth be told.
I just knew it was going to be a really long one,
So I kept on postponing and putting it on hold.

But now, my laptop has succumbed to the whim,
Of Microsoft's latest time-taker-upper.
The pc has turned itself off and on and off and on again,
I dare not look away and make myself a cuppa.

"Working on update. 33 per cent complete.
This might take a while", it cruelly mocks.
For half an hour, it's displayed this same fabrication.
It's like a full-on technical cleanse and detox.

I sincerely hope that 33 per cent is the new 99 per cent,
Because it hasn't changed in twenty minutes or more.
Has the hard drive frozen or fallen into inertia?
Perhaps, a more serious issue deep down in its core?

At last, a slight alteration in the screen text,
The process is now 50 per cent complete.
I'm hoping that the remaining half is more speedy,
Because I don't want the whole unit to overheat.

"99 per cent complete", we're almost there,
My laptop will be back in full working order soon.
I can't go through this time-consuming nonsense again,
I'll have to change the setting to "once in a blue moon".

* * *

JURY'S OUT

Four times have I been called for jury service at Crown Court,
While others my age haven't been summoned even once.
My civic duty has requested a total of eight weeks of my time,
Although I have been reimbursed a nice bit of bunce.

The jury assembly room is filled with people from all walks of life,
Many of whom complain about being picked for the service.
But a judicial system without 12 men and women good and true,
Would, if *they* were on trial, make them a tad more nervous.

I was picked for a trial, and without mentioning the details,
It was a farce from the first minute to the last.
Firstly, the prosecuting council forgot all of his notes,
So, the judge gave him a stare, then an icy verbal blast.

And following the summing up, the jury returned to our room.
Only to find a slew of unsubmitted evidence in the juror's file.
So, instead of pondering the guilt of the man in the dock.
We told the judge who ordered an immediate retrial.

Then, on day two of a trial for firearms offences,
A fellow juror was forced into admitting to her peers,
That the accused was known to her and her family,
As he went out with her daughter for almost two years.

I was elected foreman of the jury as I was an old hand,
A responsibility I felt humbled, but eager to take.
Especially when the tea order was placed with an usher-
It was my decision to choose all the pastries and the cake.

Back in the courtroom, all present tried not to laugh,
As an old Cockney fellow gave his version of events.
The judge warned him not to use rhyming slang,
"Upholding the language of the East End", was no defence.

One of my fellow jurors had me wondering in concern,
Would I want *my* fate decided by someone so cruel?
She'd hang the accused because 'his eyes are too close together'.
Instead of weighing up the evidence; the ignorant fool.

Of course, sometimes one has to wait in the assembly area,
For days on end without once being called to sit.
Then the boredom sets in, and the complaining ramps up,
From those who wished they hadn't agreed to commit.

I maintain that serving on a jury is one's duty.
It's something to be embraced in a just society.
Especially if one is elected as foreman of the jury,
With the task to decide the patisserie variety.

* * *

THE JOY OF HOME SHOPPING

My days of pushing wonky trollies down the aisles are over,
I've finally woken up to the joy of home shopping.
No more spaces to find in huge busy car parks,
And getting delayed behind shoppers starting and stopping.

I just get the old laptop out and log on to the site,
And a world of food and provisions are there.
I don't want to sound like an advertisement here-
But it can all be done from the comfort of your armchair.

OK, there won't be all the offers you normally find,
And the range might not be quite as extensive.
And you'll probably buy things you don't even need,
So your 'visit' might be slightly more expensive.

The one small quirk that can get a little annoying,
Is the substitution of items that don't seem valid.
A dozen eggs for a 'different' dozen eggs is fine,
But why do they think coleslaw is the same as potato salad?

However, another little blip has occurred in recent weeks,
No marmite in. I miss that black gloop so much.
Of course, I could just nip to a local shop to buy a jar,
But that's giving in, and I refuse to be a soft touch.

Reserving a delivery slot and completing an order,
Is a satisfying, almost gratifying process for me.
Far better than loading and unloading bags from my car.
And well worth the delivery charge of one pound and seventy-five pee.

The most annoying thing, I no longer have to suffer,
For me, was worse than everything else combined-
Was the realisation as soon as I reached the cashier,
That I'd once again left my wallet behind.

On the whole, the experience is a pleasurable one,
I never again want to go on a supermarket jolly.
And if there is just one thing that makes it all worthwhile,
It's not having to find a pound for that blasted wonky trolley.

* * *

INJURY LAWYERS FOR ME

I've had an accident that wasn't my fault. So who's going to help me?
There must be a firm who'll take up a case for my poor shattered knee.
It happened in the workplace, so that certainly ticks one box.
But it wasn't in normal work hours, so that could create a paradox.
The boss didn't safely store away the ladder that I was using,
And that was the reason for my wound and widespread bruising.
I needed the steps to get down from the window of the storeroom,
That I'd climbed through dressed in my all-black costume.
I wanted to *liberate* some electrical goods... to give to the poor,
It was their negligence, leaving a trail of forklift grease on the floor!
That's why the ladder I was using wasn't able to grip,
And that's why I fell, making my journey a one-way trip.
It's my legal right to sue them. It's a heinous health and safety issue.
Look what their carelessness did to my patella and surrounding tissue.
So, I'm going to call a firm, which I hope might end my hell,
Before recreation hour ends and it's back to my prison cell.

* * *

MY OBJECTION TO REJECTION

My email inbox holds yet another rejection,
From an agent snubbing my poetry collection.
It's hard not to feel total and utter dejection,
Although I begrudgingly accept, it's down to subjection.

I have tried to create a literary connection,
Between myself and an agent in a positive direction.
But so far, all I've received is very little affection,
For my work, which has failed to make a lasting impression.

I'll review my offering and make the odd correction,
Perhaps I'll need to slightly alter the inflexion.
Or maybe collate them into a rigid subsection,
To attract interest, concluding a careful inspection.

A little fine-tuning might change the complexion,
Perchance, I'll receive positivity without objection.
To dilute this desperate feeling of disaffection,
From those who insist on literary perfection.

* * *

JUNK MAIL

In this age of recycling and cutting down on waste,
The amount of junk mail I get is a joke in bad taste.
Leaflets for cuisines from Lebanon to Bulgaria,
And the pizza parlour that doesn't deliver to my area.

Regular contributors to my blue recycling bin include–
New shops in town, selling milkshakes and vegan food.
Estate agent flyers almost *begging* me to sell my home,
And one from a local farm selling non-GM honeycomb.

"Babysitting and nannying services. Call this number…"
"Mattresses under half price. Improve your slumber."
"We'll get your garden ready for the barbecue season.
Money-back guarantee if you're not satisfied (within reason)."

If I needed a solicitor, I wouldn't call "Dave from Mill Hill",
And I wouldn't use the services of "Pat the fat VAT man", with free will.
Reconditioned Georgian style furniture would be wasted on me,
And as for the bloke down the road trying to sell a rusty Ford Capri…

Apart from a monthly bank statement and occasional HMRC mail,
The amount of mail which is junk I get is practically off the scale.
I should probably fix a paper shredder to the inside of my front door.
That would save me needlessly filling up the kitchen drawer.

Don't get me wrong; people can advertise what they like,
Apart from the rude driveway bloke, he can go take a hike.
It's just the sheer volume that I receive on a daily basis,
That makes me wish for a future of a junk mail free oasis.

* * *

THIS POLITICAL LIFE

There are not many of us who will sympathise with the plight,
Of a member of the British parliament who resigns and takes flight,
Following an inquiry finding them guilty of fiddling expenses.
The journey back from the political abyss will require mending fences.

From Opposition front bench spokesperson to a Government cabinet
minister,
Or a backbench stalwart, there's usually something quite sinister,
At the way they justify their conduct amidst dodgy business affairs,
Hoping that the public won't rumble them and that nobody even cares.

Speaking of affairs, extra-marital liaisons, have always been rife,
When ministers are "hard" in Westminster, away from the wife.
For some Secretaries of State, the chance to connect with an aide,
In an unused office, beneath a CCTV camera, simply cannot be
delayed.

Over the years, scandals involving finance and coercion,
Have gone hand-in-hand with those of sexual perversion.
But should we be surprised at an MP's disdain for the voter—
Whether they bury their transgressions or they're a serial
self-promoter?

But it's not only Members of Parliament who, towards the public,
simply scoff.
At local council level too, snouts are buried deep in the trough.
They benefit from awarding building contracts to pals in the trade,
Accepting "consultancy fees" from spurious organisations in the shade.

I don't doubt that many enter politics for the right reason,
But most end up making hay long before the end of their first season.
I'm more than happy to tar them all with the same brush,
Because, if they played poker, they'd somehow draw a Royal Flush.

* * *

A BIDET-FUL OF BOOKS

Once it was a small sample of brochures and the odd magazine,
Now, a stack of books reside in my bidet, still on the increase.
They have found a home nestled in the redundant bowl,
Beside the toilet, my seat of learning, knowledge and peace.

It started with a takeaway menu and an invitation to the AA,
Which were soon joined by an Ikea catalogue and a wedding invite.
And before I knew it, the first sports quiz book found a place,
Giving me some questions to ponder as day became night.

The first novel to join the paperback assemblage was by John Grisham.
However, I can't remember which one it was though -
It could well have been The Juror or maybe The Pelican Brief.
Then it could just as easily have been The Client or Calico Joe.

Alongside the paperbacks, junk mail and gutter cleaning leaflets,
Reference books then joined the collection at great speed -
And even the hard-backed Complete Works of Shakespeare,
Something that I would dip into, but I'm not studious enough to read.

The time I spend on the throne is, without doubt, increasing,
And I'm not even through a quarter of the literature at hand.
So, I've taken to having long baths instead of quick showers,
In order to read the books just like I'd once planned.

But, the sheer volume of material is getting larger,
And it's time to free up the white porcelain space.
To relieve it of pamphlets, paperbacks and manuals,
In readiness to begin the whole process again, at pace.

* * *

LITTLE JAR OF PICKLES

I pick up the little jar of pickles from the back of the fridge,
It has been a mainstay of the middle shelf, for sure.
Even longer than the shallots, the beetroot and the chutney,
The numerous half-empty jars of jam and more.

In fact, it may have made its way from the old fridge,
That cooled its last at the start of the decade.
And has been left pickling, waiting to be chosen,
Never the bride, always the bridesmaid.

The seal is still intact, and the contents still look fresh,
As I pondered if it's time to release the contents within,
But I quickly put it back to the place where it stays,
Besides the half bottle of Gordon's sloe gin.

There it will rest, the master of all it surveys,
Alone and cold– the condiment no one has desired.
No burger, no salad, no sandwich comes a-calling.
Will these green, nobly pickles ever be required?

It seems unlikely that the seal will be broken.
And when the fridge next has a spring clean,
That lonely, little jar of unwanted, unloved pickles,
Will be discarded and finally depart the scene.

* * *

LOTTERY THRILL

I've played since the first day it started,
Without scooping a significant win.
The same one line with the same six numbers,
My winnings so far have been very thin.

A tenner here and a tenner there,
Were the only prizes to come my way.
Then they cruelly increased the number of balls,
Thus decreasing my chances; I called "foul play".

Still, occasionally some numbers do come up,
And an email notification I'll receive.
Quoting -"We have news for you. You've won a prize!"
Then a wild tapestry of expectation, I'll weave.

If I see that mail waiting in my inbox at night,
I'll wait until the morning, using caution and stealth.
Giving me a few hours to ponder and dream,
About what I'll do with my newfound wealth.

A new car or two would be the starting point,
But how will they fit in the drive?
I'll have to buy a bigger house with the rest of the dosh,
Just large enough to park four or five.

I'll wake up from my dreams of fantastic wealth,
And consider the National Lottery's unopened mail.
'I could be a millionaire at this very moment.'
My excited curiosity, I try to curtail.

I open the mail and follow the link,
And sign in to my lottery account.
"Congratulations, you've matched three numbers!"
Twenty-five pounds was the lowly amount.

My new millionaire lifestyle will have to be put on hold,
At least, until the next draw, later in the week.
Besides, I don't need the hassle of moving home,
And to an estate agent, I won't need to speak.

My old car will have the run of the driveway,
Unencumbered by a newer, shinier arrival.
And my bank balance will stay barely be in the black,
Thus felicitating my continued survival.

Next time, I think, when I receive a lottery email,
I'll open it immediately- I shan't pause or hesitate.
Maybe, just maybe, I'll hit all six numbers
Although, with my luck, a mere lucky dip will be my fate.

* * *

HANG 'EM OUT TO DRY

The calling by the press and other media,
For government resignations baffles me.
Why should the incompetence of these errant ministers,
Be "rewarded" by the release of culpability?

Firing is seen as the ultimate consequence.
I disagree and find it hard to comprehend,
The call to "sack" them by the red top press.
'Explain your actions!' -that's what I recommend.

A couple of years of skulking on the backbenches,
And preserving their ministerial pension,
Is hardly a just and worthy punishment.
It's certainly beyond my comprehension.

A ministerial decision or complete of lack one,
Followed by the inevitable cover-up attempt,
Should at least trigger a public explanation,
Showcasing the extent of the MP's contempt.

Publicly humiliate these dreadful miscreants,
In front of the people they laughingly represent.
And force them to explain on national TV,
The scandalous reasons behind their intent.

Some would say that this won't stop their shenanigans,
They'd just increase their determination not to get caught.
That may be true, but wouldn't it be good to know,
That a lesson would inevitably be taught?

* * *

GETTING THROUGH MAN FLU

'Do you want anything to eat?' my wife enquires.
'I don't think I could eat a morsel,''I moan from my bed.
'OK. If you want anything later, just shout... if you can.'
'Maybe just a couple slices of toast... use the wholemeal bread.'

'Do you want anything on it, or do you want it plain?'
'I don't think I could stomach anything on top.
Well, perhaps a smear of peanut butter if we have some.
If not, would you mind just nipping up to the shop?'

I prop myself up and let out a pained yelp.
'Just switch on the TV, Sky Sports, please.
Not too loud though, my head's in agony.
You wouldn't believe the pain when I sneeze.'

"How's your throat today? Does it still hurt?
Any better than last night?" she asks with a smile.
'It's no better. It's terribly painful,' I inform her.
'I'll just have to put up with it, at least for a while.'

'You poor thing. It must be horrific,' says my wife.
"You have no idea", I reply with a cough.
'I must remain strong and get through this hell.
Ooh, pass my phone, will you, before you get off?'

'Is there anything else you need from the shop?
Any tablets, medicine or more pain relief?'
'Just a newspaper and some fruit pastilles if you could,
Oh, and see if they have any sliced roast beef.'

'And when you come back, telephone my folks,
I don't have the strength to call them.
If they heard me try to speak, they'd only worry.
And I don't want to keep bringing up phlegm.'

'I don't mean to be a pest, but I've never felt so bad,'
I tell my wife, "I hope I'll make it until next week.'
'Oh, I'm sure you will," she says, straightening the duvet.
'How do you manage with things looking so bleak?'

Some women simply mock and don't understand,
Just how debilitating flu can be to a man.
It's not like we're making up the terrible effects,
Like it's some well thought out and deceiving plan.

'I'll be off now,' my wife says from the bedroom door.
'Just you rest, take it easy and stay put.
I might be a little while longer than usual,' she continues.
'It's not easy to walk with this broken foot.'

* * *

CHRISTMAS DAY MORN

The pattern of events is the same,
Although now we start after nine.
My teens no longer wake at the crack of dawn,
Their beds are their sole confine.

But as soon as they have awoken,
To the living room, we all convene,
Where two individual piles of presents,
Are stacked up, all neat and pristine.

I'll toss a coin to see who starts first,
In the great gift unwrapping project.
The kids gleefully rip off the colourful paper,
And their presents they'll happily inspect.

They weren't always as disciplined, of course,
It was a virtual free-for-all a few years ago.
Little hands and arms everywhere under the tree,
To find out what Santa has delivered from his grotto.

In two towers, the gifts are then re-piled,
Along with tags or cards to identify the giver.
So the children know where they came from,
And a thank you call, they'll later deliver.

Educational toys, board games and DVDs,
Have made way for video games and other tech stuff.
But the excitement of receiving an unexpected gift,
Still shows on their faces; that's thanks enough.

When all the presents have been revealed,
The first clean up task of the day can begin.
Ripped open envelopes and balls of old wrap,
Are introduced to a black sack and discarded within.

The Christmas chocolate variety packs are opened,
And its contents are scattered around in haste.
Because there's something about eating chocolate at Christmas,
That curiously does much to improve the taste.

For many years we'd tuck into breakfast,
When Christmas began at the break of day.
But in modern times, and due to the later start,
A plethora of snacks keeps the hunger at bay.

Whether we visit family or spend Christmas at home,
The traditional morning ritual remains the same.
Presents, chocolates and and a handful of nuts or ten,
Before luncheon commences, to critical acclaim.

* * *

A JOYLESS JACKPOT

4.30 am and when most players have dispersed,
A glamorous lady sits alone at a high stakes slot.
She repetitively feeds the machine with dollar bills,
In the hope that one spin will reveal the jackpot.

I arrived in Las Vegas just yesterday morning,
And the local time I hadn't yet adjusted to.
The hotel casino is quiet, and punters sparse,
Just a few stragglers and the cleaners walk through.

I'm sitting at the bar; my eyes fixed on the lady,
Elegantly perched in sunglasses and designer clothes.
Spin after spin, win a bit, lose a bit,
Seldom breaking her solemn repose.

A waitress delivers her a drink on a tray.
A vodka or perhaps a Bacardi with a slice.
She knocks it back, and the glass is returned,
Leaving behind just a large chunk of ice.

The woman presents a twenty-dollar bill,
Which the waitress accepts with a smile.
She is dismissed and quickly departs the scene,
With elegance and a certain amount of guile.

With a scratch of her nose and a lick of the lips,
The determined gambler continues her quest.
She carefully dips into her open handbag,
Without an emotion on her face expressed.

The machine takes more cash, and down comes a hand,
On the large red button, starting another spin.
Every now and then, a jaunty tune will play,
Indicating a modest but significant win.

The scene is getting evermore repetitive,
And I think it is high time I retired to bed.
But all of a sudden and without any warning,
A fanfare from the machine is despread.

The jackpot has finally been achieved.
The lady should be shaking with delight,
But instead, she remains in a stoic posture,
Amidst a wild display of flashing, golden light.

An attendant comes to her assistance,
And confirms the prize she has won.
Within a few minutes, he's back with a wad of cash,
But on the lady's face, emotion, there is none.

My heart is beating fast in excitement,
But the winner remains in the same pose.
As bill after bill is placed in her hand,
There's just another slight scratch of the nose.

I can't say for sure how much her winnings are,
But it looks like thousands from where I'm sitting,
I know I'd be cheering and whooping in elation,
Making a right scene, British reserve, permitting.

At the machine, the lady continues her session,
As if nothing had happened moments before.
She begins pumping her newly gained fortune,
Into the slot, like it was an everyday chore.

But, there are no more jaunty tunes,
And no more flashes of luminescent bliss.
The machine recoups its considerable wealth,
Something the lady is happy to dismiss.

How odd must it be to win or lose,
Without sadness, regret or delight.
To score a huge sum of money on a game of luck,
And it meaning nothing; for me, it's not right.

I don't know if this lady is wealthy beyond belief,
Or she's an addict who simply can't stop.
Perhaps she's spending her children's inheritance,
Or her ex-husband's alimony whilst in a strop.

Whatever the reason is for her blank expression,
Into the gambling precipice, *I* will never fall.
If I stuck ten bucks in a slot and took out a ton–
Well, I'd be more than happy with that little haul.

So, I stand up from my chair and leave the casino,
Just turning back to take one more glance,
At the poor, rich woman sitting at her machine,
Forlorn, emotionless, in a trance.

* * *

FIRST DAY OF SPRING

The first day of spring, whenever that may be,
Awakens the country from months-long sleep.
Within minutes of the sun appearing in a clear blue sky,
Out come the nation's gardeners; lawns ready to upkeep.

Then the hedge trimmers see some urgent action,
An incessant drone begins in haste.
From every direction, there's a constant buzzing,
In case the weather turns, there's not a moment to waste.

Radiators still on, but with open windows,
The heat and cool breeze contest the fight.
The occupants of each household caught in limbo,
All because they've glimpsed a little sunlight.

With lengthening days, old clichés abound,
'You know, this time last week, it was dark,'
Is the annual cry of the eternal optimist.
Already planning for picnics in the park.

The first wasp of the year keeps bashing its head,
As you watch it try to fly through the pane,
Of the only window that you've left unopened,
As it predictably begins to rain.

The grey clouds return to blot out the sun,
The first day of spring was misread.
The windows close, and the radiators glow.
And the lawnmowers return to the shed.

* * *

SALTED CARA-HELL

Am I the only one who doesn't get
The salted caramel thing in chocolate,
Ice cream and breakfast spread?

Where did it come from?
And where's it going to stop?
It's something I've become to dread.

They put it in hot chocolate
And in milkshakes as well.
It's even a flavour now in coffee.

Who thought it a good idea
To put salt in a sweet treat?
They've even started sticking it in toffee.

You'll find it in sauces
And cake icing too.
You can't escape the horrible stuff.

Sometimes it's subtle,
Sometimes it's overpowering,
The idea of it leaves me feeling rough.

It can flavour sweet popcorn,
Cakes, brownies and cookies,
And the top of profiteroles and eclairs too.

Salted caramel has arrived,
It's in and on everything,
Even served hot and melted in a fondue.

I know it's not essential
To consume the stuff I hate,
I've even begun to dislike its sickly salty smell.

But I fear it's not a fad,
Or just a "flavour of the month.'"
That dastardly, despicable salted caramel.

* * *

FREE FROM

I guess I'm kind of fortunate,
I don't have ongoing trials,
When at my local supermarket,
And walking down the aisles.

A I complete my weekly shop,
I don't have to stop and inspect,
Packets, boxes and containers,
For warnings, however hard to detect.

I am not a vegan. I don't keep Kosher,
And I'm able to eat all things dairy.
Peanuts, caffeine and shellfish are all fine-
My eating preferences are purely arbitrary.

I'm not gluten or lactose intolerant.
I eat pretty much anything, for my crimes.
I'm neither caffeine or fructose intolerant either.
I'm just plain intolerant at times.

I don't need products to be rice-free.
I don't need products to be nut-free.
I don't need products to be sodium-free.
However, do draw the line at them being taste-free.

I think it's truly marvellous,
That shops cater for all of society,
Whose allergies and aversions,
Would once limit their food variety.

Of course, we all want to eat healthily,
And buy food that does us good.
But, the only label I'd like to find,
Says "cost-free" – then again… I would.

* * *

BIN COLLECTION DAY

It starts in earnest the night before –
The evening hours filled with the sound,
Of little black wheels, trundling over,
The hard concrete and stone of the ground.

Ending with the crash of plastic on plastic,
As the wheelie bins are smashed together,
Uniformly at the end of everyone's driveway,
In snow, sleet or whatever the weather.

In the night hours, they silently wait,
For the stop/start roar of the truck,
That starts its rounds at 8 am,
Or much earlier, if you're out of luck.

Weaving carefully down the road,
Badly parked cars they try not to disturb,
Of the residents who unsocially distance,
Their vehicles two feet from the kerb.

He used to be called a dustman-
The hi-vis waistcoat-wearing bloke.
Now we must call him a 'household waste operative.'
This political correctness is a bit of a joke.

Sometimes it's the black bin that's taken first,
On other occasions, he'll grab the blue.
It depends if the truck's destination is the landfill,
Or the recycling plant it's heading to.

Not that it matters to one "bin man,"
Who likes to get rid of the lot in one hit.
He'll load up either colour wheelie bin,
And fills the "dust cart" with any old shit.

With the truck disappearing into the distance,
And trash receptacles strewn all over the place,
The cacophony of them being put back starts in earnest,
Until the following week's wheelie bin race.

* * *

THE KITCHEN DRAWER

The kitchen drawer that's full to bursting,
Of all the things we just can't throw away,
Is something that we all have in our homes,
But the day I sort mine out is today.

I first need to sift out all the useless stuff,
Which is much easier said than done.
There's bound to be a few hidden gems in there -
Like this empty lighter shaped like a gun.

I pick up a collection of old take away menus,
And stare at the full extent of my task.
How did I manage to acquire so much junk?
Oh, at least I've found that lost face mask.

A broken window lock and a car wash token,
Are the first to be salvaged from the mess.
A sticky boiled sweet, an adventure golf pencil,
And a receipt for my daughter's prom dress.

A box of paracetamol that expired years ago,
A bottle of eye drops of similar vintage,
An empty cheque book, a pebble, a bottle top,
And some foreign coins of high mintage.

Some odd shirt buttons and a replacement zip,
Might become useful one day.
However, I've thought that for many years,
When that excuse wasn't such a cliché.

The badge from the Olympics in 2012,
Could be a collector's item in a few years' time.
But on closer inspection, the pin is absent,
And it's caked in a translucent slime.

An invitation to a wedding, I fondly remember,
A beautiful union; universally endorsed.
"A marriage made in heaven," everyone agreed.
Such a pity the couple are now divorced.

A bent letter opener, a piece of wallpaper,
Picture hooks and two odd shoelaces.
A long, rusty screw, a reel of pink thread,
And a pack of playing cards without any aces.

Elastic bands so old they've become brittle,
A few stray staples and two 12p stamps,
Stuck to the base with some renegade glue,
Along with plug fuses, assorted amps.

A yellow Post-it note clings to the side,
With a phone number faded with time.
With no clues to whom it belongs,
I try to remember, but no bells chime.

And the inevitable old pair of glasses,
Abandoned a good few years ago.
Why on earth would I need them again?
P'raps, they're a part of me I can't let go.

A bottle of sunscreen and a single black glove-
Aren't they items that everyone needs?
On the one hand, it might be cold outside,
But on the other, you could be sweating beads.

The pièce de résistance is the key collection,
That's taken me years to accrue.
Some, I'm sure, were here when we moved in,
Just what they open, I haven't a clue.

A selection of Mortices, Yales and Chubbs,
Ah, fond memories of a bygone age.
I've kept these mementoes of old front doors,
For what reason, I can't begin to gauge.

With a sharp intake of breath, I position myself,
And firmly pull the drawer out with a yank.
I proceed to tip the contents into the bin,
It's all gone, and I'm the person to thank.

Now, the drawer will have a new use,
And trash won't be allowed to collect.
It'll be home for things that need fixing,
I'm determined it won't be left unchecked.

I clean the drawer and slide it back,
Into the space from whence it came.
And immediately begin the cycle again,
By throwing in a damaged photo frame.

* * *

SEVENTEEN, BLACK

'Did you see that? The ball popped out,
Of seventeen, black, of that, there's no doubt.'
Before that wheel spun, I was so sure,
My losing streak was over; a loser, no more.
But it teased me and mocked me, made me feel a fool,
Seventeen was so welcoming to that little ball.
It knocked on the door and was invited to stay,
Just for a while so that I could make hay.
But it changed its course; to a neighbour it chose,
To thirty-four, red, and there it froze.
The guy to my side, whooped and delighted,
'My number's come in!' He was so damned excited.
'Happy for you, man,' I choked with a sneer.
'My chips have all gone. I'm getting outta here.'
I'd been conspired against; I felt sick and unstable.
As I stood up from my seat and left the table,
'Cause my misfortune continued; my legs went slack,
As I heard the croupier announce, 'Seventeen, black.'

* * *

FUEL GAUGE

Your glass can always be half full,
But you leave your fuel gauge on the red.
And the pessimistic "glass half empty" drinker,
Panics when the needle is halfway, instead.

There are folk who fill up regularly each week,
And there are those who wait until they are told-
'Go out and put some petrol in the car,'
For the fifth time by the lady of the household.

And eventually I will, just to bring about peace,
Even though the only place I've taken the car,
Is to the petrol station and back a week before,
To fill up because I fancied a sneaky Mars bar.

I barely managed a fiver's worth in the tank,
I tried, but it wouldn't take any more.
My wife is happy, and the needle's back on full.
I just can't wait for next week's encore.

* * *

TAKEAWAY NIGHT

It's takeaway night; the dance begins.
The family start their earnest perusal,
Of the menus taken from the kitchen drawer.
There's more than enough to bamboozle.

Says Dad: 'I don't want Indian again.
We've had it now, twice in a row.
And I couldn't stand another dodgy chicken tikka-
My stomach just cannot handle the woe.'

Says Mum: 'And I've gone right off Chinese.
They've been going downhill of late.
We always order too much in any event,
And I leave most of it right on my plate.'

Says son: 'Well, I don't want a kebab again.
The donner's too greasy and the shish, too tough.
And I don't like anything else they do,
Apart from the humus, but that won't be enough.'

Says daughter: 'Before anyone suggests fish and chips, don't.
I hate batter, and their chips are too soggy.
And how can anyone eat those horrible mushy peas,
Without leaving the table feeling groggy?'

'Can I suggest Japanese?' asks Dad.
Non-enthusiastic murmurs meet the notion.
'Turkish? Moroccan? Middle-eastern food then?'
The family quickly dismiss the motion.

'And if you're thinking of McDonald's...' Dad continues.
The children sit up and whoop in delight.
The face of the elder dampens their joy,
'You can forget it; we're not having *that* tonight.'

"How about we try that new Vegan restaurant?"
Mum's suggestion draws a blank from the rest.
"I'd rather eat these menus than go there,"
Says Dad, quickly dismissing his wife's request.

The family sit bereft of further ideas,
To agree on what to eat, they were unable.
'Well, last night's leftover lasagne it is then,' announced Mum.
Sighs of disappointment emit from around the table.

* * *

WHO'S NEXT?

I've stood behind this counter for many a year,
Lending dough to my punters to pay rent and buy beer.
Fireman, nurses, gamblers and whores,
They've all entered this shop through those big glass doors.

Who's next? That bloke with hundred and one dodgy chains,
Or the tube driver from Bow, who's frightened of trains?
That fresh-faced young girl with a brooch, newly stolen,
Or the kindly old pensioner with the spastic colon?

What about that old fusspot who lives over the pub,
Or the teenage mother who's always in the club?
The Romanian, The Pole, The Latvian, The Scot –
Three of them I understand– the last, I do not.

The family of travellers from across the water,
Or the creepy, tall guy whose wife is his daughter?
I jest about that; she's too smart for that mister,
But they look so alike, so she could be his sister.

Maybe it'll be the schoolteacher, all glamour and glitz,
Who came in last week and flashed me her… smile.
Did she really think that I would offer her more-
For her chunky yellow bangle with the stainless steel core?

Perhaps, the sweet old man whose pension's always late?
Alongside his friend, the woman with the ever-balding pate.
Or the fake Mafia Godfather who is always broke,
Because he gives all his money to help the old folk.

How 'bout that funny barber, who is regularly plastered-
He likes to come for a chat, the drunk old bastard.
Geordie Mac, Big Phil, Bullshit Billy or Miss Old,
Come bring me your fake rings, which you claim are gold.

I can never forget Babs, the flirty old broad,
Who made an absolute mint from her third husband's fraud,
Then she blew the lot, lost on five-card draw.
Now, she's on the prowl for hubby number four.

The good, the bad and the utterly crazy,
The genial geriatric who makes me jalfrezi.
They all bring colour and spice to my job.
What would I do without that mad mob?

But where are they now, my eclectic troop?
I kind of miss them and feel out of the loop.
I'll just wait for them calmly, and I won't get vexed.
Ready to greet them and ask, 'Who's next?'

* * *

CINEMA ETIQUETTE

It's not the price of tickets that puts me off,
Or even the cost of popcorn and drinks.
It's not even due to the difficulty in parking,
It's the filmgoer's behaviour that stinks.

I don't mind the constant crinkling of wrappers,
Or people slurping on Fanta or Coke.
The crimes I refer to are far more heinous,
And malevolent feelings inside me evoke.

I'm talking about the curse of mobile phones,
Not so much the beeps, buzzes and rings.
It's the shard of bright light piercing the darkness,
And the disturbance to my enjoyment it brings.

I think most have heeded the regular warnings,
To switch their phones off; at least put them on mute.
But the inability to leave the blasted thing alone,
I'm afraid my mind cannot compute.

Those flashes of light in the blackness,
Like car headlights beaming at night.
Appear from all corners of the theatre,
Causing me to feel angry and uptight.

I long for the days of just chewing and crunching,
I had learnt the skills to ignore all that.
Along with rustling, coughing and the clearing of throats,
Even the annoying murmurs of mindless chit chat.

Please try and resist for a couple of hours-
Friends on Facebook and WhatsApp will have to wait,
To be informed that you're watching a film whilst on the phone.
Though, I understand how that sacrifice will frustrate.

* * *

A FAN-LESS GAME

Football, football, everywhere, but not a fan in sight.
Performing in front of empty stands was a player's lockdown plight.
Gone was the matchday experience, for folks across the nation,
No support from match-going fans; it was soccer's biggest frustration.

Uneaten hot dogs and undrunk beer,
Quiet terraces bereft of song and cheer.
Players' shouts and screams, the only sounds,
In the eerie atmosphere of empty grounds.

On TV, there was a plethora of matches to view.
Dozens of games a week, we had to get through.
From Europe, the Prem; down to the National League,
It was no surprise that viewers felt an air of fatigue.

Courtesy of BT, Amazon, The Beeb, and Sky,
We were bombarded by soccer, although some did decry,
The hours we spent watching the games on TV.
Perhaps they preferred to watch reruns of Glee?

To the stadiums and grounds we longed to get back.
To listen to the familiar weekend soundtrack,
Of those songs and cheers from jubilant fans,
And the return to football and regular plans.

But that was when we were only able,
To watch the game via Freeview, satellite or cable.
But watching footie on TV is not a patch,
On experiencing the joy of being back at the match.

* * *

A SUSPICION OF SUPERSTITION

Millions of prayers have been said, and many more will be made.
Promises they can stay up late to every Jordan, Jude and Jade.

Thousands of lucky pants laid out to be worn.
Superstitions are in overdrive on Euro 2020 final morn.

The same breakfast on the same plate has been eaten today.
For the sake of continuity and to keep bad omens at bay.

More butterflies in more stomachs than in a thousand sunny fields.
A day for even the haters to lower their emotional shields.

Beards having been grown since the 11th of June.
"Three Lions" sung loudly, no matter how out of tune.

The same seat is claimed whether at home or in the pub.
The familiar selection for the pre-match drink and grub.

Saying the same phrases at the same time, "just for fun".
Just because they've been said every time England won.

The Wimbledon Men's Singles Final, a mere sporting sideshow.
The main event starts at 8, but it's a nice little combo.

At 7 o'clock, of course, choosing BBC One over ITV.
Like we've always done; not many would disagree.

Chomping a handful of Twiglets with a swig of pink gin.
As has been done before every previous England win.

And so it finally begins, the kick-off at Wembley,
Ossie's the only one whose knees aren't going trembly.

An unbreakable belief that "Cometh the men, cometh the hour".
Deals having been brokered with a higher (or a lower) power.

All that matters now is to win that trophy by fair way or theft.
Is football coming home? For me, it never left.

* * *

CHANGING PHOTOS

Changing framed photos of the kids in my house,
   Can really put my marriage to the test.
   The constant adding to the collection,
   Can leave me confused and quite stressed.

I'll hover my hand over a photo, and I'll be told,
'You can't change the baby ones', and 'that one stays there,'
   Any argument of mine falls of deaf ears;
   I bite my lip and do my best not to swear.

'We just haven't the room for *all* of the photos.'
   I attempted to validate my point of view.
   'It's not like we don't see the kids every day.'
   After a stern stare, my point, I withdrew.

Space now is at such a premium,
   On the windowsill in my living room.
   With photos from the last fifteen years,
   Although a drawer full of others still loom.

In the past, I've tried to be a sneaky.
Leaving the ones that the kids appear as a pair.
To keep the volume of individual faces the same,
Then secreted some other photos elsewhere.

But that worked for all of a day,
And when I returned from a night out with friends,
Back they all were – all the hidden pics and frames,
And then some more, as if to make amends.

I admit, there's no doubt about it,
A bigger house we will need.
Or at least I'll have to put up some more shelves,
I have little option but to concede.

So, with the number of photos ever-growing,
Plans to free up space, I've had to scrap.
And there are now so many images of my children,
That they have now begun to overlap.

* * *

THE FA CUP FINAL SIDESHOW

What has happened to the FA Cup final?
It used to be *the* sporting event of the year.
The culmination of a season of soccer–
An occasion the whole nation held dear.

On the morning, I would rush to the newsagent,
To buy a match day programme for the big event.
Even though *my* team rarely took part,
I'd joyfully paw through the entire content.

The dedicated build-up began at midday,
To the final, the BBC and ITV devoted hours,
To FA Cup related quiz shows and features,
And both teams' progress to the Twin Towers.

From a team bus on the way to Wembley,
Cameras would take us on board to view,
Men in matching tracksuits, sporting perms,
Fooling around, acting the goat, right on cue.

Of course, they were trying to shield us,
From their feelings of nervous tension.
As the coach arrived on Wembley Way,
The atmosphere was one of apprehension.

The nerves were building at home as well.
You didn't have to support a team taking part.
Then the lineups were announced, in those days,
We knew every single player who would start.

The feature event of the footballing calendar,
Kicked off at 3 pm, it was set in stone.
After Abide With, and then the National Anthem,
It was unlike anything the players had known.

But all that took place many years ago now,
It was a purer and more innocent age.
When an FA Cup winners' medal really meant something,
To the competitors on football's biggest stage.

To score a goal in the cup final was an incredible feat,
The very pinnacle of many player's careers.
You could see in their faces just what it meant,
A joy replicated by all his colleagues and peers.

But today the match begins at half five.
And it is sandwiched between two Premier League games.
It's not even the last day of the domestic season,
The broadcasters and the FA must share the blame.

Replays have long since been abandoned,
No second match to determine the winners.
Instead, a penalty shootout, where the ones who miss,
Will forever be painted as sinners.

It's a means to an end, a mere gateway to Europe,
And not even the premier competition at that.
A spot in the Europa League, alongside the minnows,
Is the reward for this diluted spectacle and format.

Fourth in the league and a Champions League berth,
Is far more important than the FA Cup now,
To the owners and chairman of the most glamorous clubs.
Because of prize money and being the sponsors' cash cow.

So, unhappily that's where we are now,
And no matter how the broadcasters try to find,
New ways to "big up" the world's oldest cup competition,
They fail miserably in this supporter's mind.

* * *

THE OLD NORMAL

They talk about the "new normal",
But, I'm not sure if I perfected the old one.
I had the "slightly odd at times" sorted,
And even had "somewhat strange"in my repertoire.
I don't think I reached the "worrying weird" stage,
But, I could "play the fool" with the best of them.
I was comfortable with "acting like a loon",
And even be accused of "behaving like a right idiot".
But I drew the line at "worrying bizarre",
Or, at least, I nudged it further away.
So, here I am giving serious consideration,
To what the "new normal" actually means.
This in itself might raise a few questions,
To those "normals", whoever they may be.

* * *

DRIVE-BY DRIVEWAY

'I'm not here today to sell you anything,'
The young man at the door lied through his teeth.
'I just want to talk to you about your driveway.'
Carefully hiding the sales patter beneath.

'Oh. That's nice. It's my favourite subject,' I said.
He didn't pick up on my sarcasm; I offered a smile.
He surveyed my pathway and nodded intently,
'Looks like you haven't had this repaved for a while.'

'I haven't had it done… ever', I blared in exaggeration.
'I wish I could afford it, but I can't, I'm afraid."
The clue to my finances made no impression,
As he opened a folder in an attempt to persuade.

'We have a selection of designs you can choose from,'
He said, showing me some plastic covered pics.
'They look great,' I said. The salesman smiled.
'And they're all free? I like the one with red bricks.'

'No, they're not free,' he said without a hint of sarcasm.
'But you said you weren't here to sell me anything,' I said.
He looked terribly confused and awfully befuddled.
'There is nothing to pay *today*. That was my thread.'

'Ahhh. Then you *do* want me to part with some money.
I wish you would have made that clear.
My hopes were raised, and now they're dashed.
And I was going to ask if you could also do the rear.'

The notion that I was, in fact, joking with him,
Finally registered on the young lad's face.
I could visibly tell he was weighing up his options,
Whether to continue his pitch or leave with grace.

I decided to put him out of his misery.
I told him I could not afford a new drive.
'Come back again in twenty years or so,
'And maybe I'll agree... if I'm still alive.'

* * *

THE WORST DAY OF THE YEAR

Another year older and more miles on the clock.
A day of apprehension; a time to take stock.
Twelve months on, with all the places I've been.
And all the things I've done, and the people I've seen.

It's not my birthday; an anniversary or owt,
It's MOT day, filled with worry and doubt.
The appointment is made, tyre treads checked,
And not a single broken brake light that I could detect.

I drive to the garage and drop off my key,
To a man in dirty overalls, holding a mug of tea.
I leave the centre and go for a walk,
I just can't hang around to watch and to gawk.

I wonder if it will fail and what it would take-
A loose connection or a slightly worn brake?
Or high exhaust emissions could be a fact,
All these worries on my mind; I can't keep track.

And if it does fail, what will it cost to put right?
Did I check the bodywork and the reverse light?
So many questions I should have addressed before.
Now, swirling around my mind, impossible to ignore.

I then return to the garage to learn my fate,
The mechanic stands before me. 'Alright, mate?
All done. I'll bring your certificate out.'
It passed! I knew it would. It was never in doubt.

* * *

"WE'RE ALL DOOMED!"

A lot of people think it's a modern thing–
All these shortages of food, fuel and manpower.
It seems we're always being warned of impending doom,
From those media bosses in their ivory tower.

As a nation, oh, how we love to panic–
A reaction magnified by broadcasters of news.
"A winter of discontent is coming", they warn us.
Attempting to colour coordinate our seasonal blues.

"Fuel rationing is arriving!" social media shrieks,
As a handful of petrol stations temporarily shut.
So queues start on forecourts all over the land,
As alarm spreads when fuel deliveries are cut.

Many older folks remember the dark days of the 70s,
Electricity rationing was amongst the government's goals.
But three-day weeks and random power outages,
Still didn't provoke us to stockpile bog rolls.

Sensationalist stories and wild, sweeping headlines,
Will compound huge swathes of people's fears.
"We're all going to hell in a carbon-neutral handbasket.
Because we've been raping our natural resources for years."

Panic buying will no doubt rear its ugly head again,
Pasta and those toilet rolls will be difficult to locate.
As you tut and shake your head at hoarding shoppers,
Before redirecting your ire to Facebook, most irate.

And then, our government loves to poke the hornet's nest,
And persist in driving home the message of despair.
But reverse psychology is their weapon of choice,
'Don't panic buy,' they repeat with great and intense fanfare.

There are those of us who still blame Brexit,
For others, Covid is the cause for all this fuss.
A sudden lack of CO_2 is the latest culprit
Or is it the government just trying to control us?

* * *

A WHITTY LITTLE DITTY

Here's a short ditty about Christopher Whitty,
The man with the ill-fitting suit.
With consummate ease, he'd say, 'next slide, please.'
And show graphs that many dispute.

Dressed like a mortician, he continued his mission,
To remind folk in every household.
With his unnerving voice, he said we've no choice,
To obey all the rules we've been told.

And with unblinking eyes, the news he'd reprise,
About rising cases in the community.
And in the interest of balance, his mate, Patrick Vallance,
Would spout exactly the same to show unity.

The kindly professor, like a computer processor,
Had a million and one facts in his head.
And good news or bad, whilst looking so sad,
He'd relay it into the camera ahead.

So, this *was* the end of the verse that I'd penned,
About the prof who was always on the box.
He looked even more bereft than the bloke to his left
The one with the stutter and blonde locks.

He's not been seen for a while, with that non-existent smile,
With Covid cases shooting up, he could soon return.
To advise every minister, no matter how sinister,
To lock down again, in a classic Government U-turn.

* * *

AN EXPENSIVE NIGHT IN

'Let's *not* go to the cinema,' my new wife suggested,
As we snuggled on the sofa, we were so closely nested.
A trip to the movies is such a colossal expense.
A cheap might at home makes far more sense.

I said, 'We can watch what we want on our 60 inch TV.'
Although who decides what to view is so rarely me.
I like panel shows, comedies, documentaries and sport,
But if I dare put the footie on, I'll be savagely cut short.

Disney Plus and Now TV, channels we have to subscribe,
Add Vimeo and Netflix too, because they're the new vibe.
Sitcoms and dramas and films and more,
So much to choose from, cherish and adore.

She went into the kitchen to make us some tea,
So, I switched to Sky Sports; at last, I was free.
For a couple of minutes, at least, I was out of jail,
The remote control in my hand; the Holy Grail.

'Turn the football off. I think it's about time,
For that terrific new drama on Amazon Prime.'
So, I sat like a good boy, and we watched some old dross,
About an American newsreader and her lecherous boss.

We should make the most of the channels we've bought,
Even though I'm not often allowed to watch much sport.
Watching the beautiful game, I'll have to suspend,
For a thousand Marvel films and box sets, no end.

So the fortune we saved on sweeties and chocs,
Will go towards the monthly bill for Britbox.
And then we'll save on hot dogs, the popcorn and Coke;
The money they charge is an absolute joke.

I'm kidding, of course, that's a drop in the ocean,
Compared to the TV and my new wife's devotion.
I'll have to sell a kidney or get a new profession,
To afford the crippling cost of "our" TV obsession.

* * *

A CHOICE OF DESSERTS

'Perhaps sir and madam would like to see the dessert menu?'
I was on a date; my first time at that particular venue.
So I casually said, 'I think we may just take a look.'
I was thinking, 'I'm having my afters, by hook or by crook!'

Even though I was pretty much stuffed after my main,
There's always room for something sweet, I maintain.
A meal without a dessert just isn't complete,
But I didn't know what to choose my post entrée treat.

I perused the innumerable choices; the selection was unreal.
There just wasn't one thing that didn't appeal,
Eton Mess, Creme Brulee and a brownie with hot fudge sauce.
Ice cream and apple pie and custard were listed, of course.

An Italian dessert- the cassata, pannacotta or tiramisu?
Or should I go for a light option, like a scoop of sorbet or two?
Something else chocolatey - the mousse, or warm fudge cake?
Mmmm, the treacle lattice tart, I could definitely partake.

The selection of cheeses and crackers sounded quite nice.
A bit of Stilton or Applewood cheddar would certainly entice.
No, definitely something sweet to finish off my meal.
But what would I have? Everything holds such appeal.

Following much deliberation and after weighing up the list,
I settled on a dish I knew couldn't be missed.
An old favourite, the crème caramel had won my vote,
Not at all heavy; it'd slip nicely down the throat.

The waiter came back, but before I could voice,
My date astounded me with *her* final choice.
'Nothing for me. Just a black coffee will do.'
'Oh, I'll have the same.' I panicked and I wished my dessert, "adieu".

What happened there? What did I say?
Too late to change my mind, the waiter took the menus away.
I still craved something sweet as we talked, sipping our coffee.
There must be something in my pocket- a wine gum or an old toffee?

'I wish I had the apple pie now,' my date belatedly sighed.
My ears pricked up as I hailed the waiter before I replied-
'Sorry, we'll have dessert after all. Creme caramel and an apple pie,
please.'
My date nodded in agreement, and I gave her hand a squeeze.

I'm sorry, sir, it's gone 11 and the kitchen's closed for the night.
Nothing was going to satisfy this fella's unfulfilled appetite.
'I've got some rocky road at home,' my date said in a seductive drawl.
I just might get my just desserts tonight, after all...'

* * *

GAME SHOW FOOLS

To me, it's an all too familiar pose.
Those clapping seals on TV game shows.
Who think that knowing their name is worth applause,
'I'm Bob, and I'm from Skipton, and I like dry stone walls.'

Then there's the laughter they like to prolong,
When they get a simple answer completely wrong.
To them, being a idiot must be so damn funny.
It's not like they want to win a large sum of money.

And there are the ones who don't *know* a lot,
They'll happily waffle on and look like a clot.
Then the best they can offer is "Er, I 'think' it might be..."
When asked, 'In the alphabet, what letter comes after 'C'?'

As for the ones who say, 'That's before my time.'
This, for me, is the contestant's biggest crime.
Especially when asked a question on modern history.
What goes through their minds, to me, is a mystery.

And why would you answer, 'I don't know.'
When given the choice of a "yes" or a "no"?
For them, I reserve my deepest contempt.
To use that line, rather an answer attempt.

Then there are the "highbrow" shows when the player on the left,
Is usually the one in the team who is totally bereft.
Of even a clue to why they are there,
And sits there uncomfortably, with a face of despair.

To hear questions you'd think were unable to botch,
Then ITV's Tipping Point is the one to watch.
To see Brenda not know what "M" comes from a cow,
Or Derek declare that a female horse is a sow.

On Pointless, each day, there are idiots galore,
Whose rank stupidity it's tough to ignore.
When a player is asked for a country ending with an "O",
Answering "Toga", his progression he'd blow.

And it's not *just* the public who are afflicted this way,
The so-called celebrities are on a similar pathway.
The faux modesty and the dearth of knowledge,
Give the distinct impression they dropped out of college.

Not every contestant can be worthy of Mastermind,
Recite the Magna Carta or be the cream of mankind.
But a little awareness and knowing a smattering of facts,
Might prevent them from getting the first round axe.

When every subject is "not one of my best,"
Then perhaps your brain is not one to test.
And risking ridicule in front of the nation,
Then maybe TV quiz shows are not your vocation.

For me, I must learn not to scream and shout,
At the contestant on TV, who is a total washout.
Perhaps they didn't spend much time at school,
And may not know there's only one F in "fool".

* * *

AMERICANISMS, NOT AMERICANIZMS

Maybe we Brits have got it all wrong,
Blaming the Americans for bad spelling.
Dropping letters here, changing letters there,
Maybe it's common sense rather than them rebelling.

Do we really need a superfluous "U",
In words like colour, valour and neighbour?
It adds nothing at all to the pronunciation,
It just adds effort to writing's labo(u)r.

They like the "S" too on the other side of the pond,
Their defense of it may cause offense over here.
But it makes perfect sense to change c's to s's,
Even though it's not the language of Will Shakespeare.

What about the final letter of the alphabet?
We call it "zed", but to them, it's simply a "zee".
They don't apologize to reorganize certain words,
The correct spelling of which, we simply can't agree.

The British also love an unnecessary "L",
When travelling, modelling and expelling.
It's just a little extra bonus we like to use,
Confusing foreigners to our way of spelling.

I'm teasing and playing devil's advocate here,
It's the English language at the end of the day.
Our way of spelling is the *right* way of spelling,
It's only a pity the Yanks don't see it that way.

* * *

NEW YEAR, NEW PANIC

First, it was toilet rolls. Why? No one really knew.

Then, pasta became the must-hoard favourite.

Rumours were rife of a nationwide rice shortage,

Which encouraged the lunatics to stock up for Armageddon.

The scramble for hand sanitiser was crazy; the black market called.

And if you could find the right type of face masks - well done!

Soap, tinned fruit and veg, even sauces were scarce.

And spaced out queues formed outside the supermarket doors.

Retailers up and down the land rationed groceries.

The grabbing hands and greedy hearts of shoppers decried–

'It's not fair. It's my right to buy a year's worth of Basmati.

And if I want to cook it with 3 litres of Carex, that's my decision.'

That was 2020, of course. The national stomach bug crisis failed to
appear.
The run on starch and carbs merely just sauntered away.
A year on and, we don't need to wash our hands anymore.
Fresh fruit and vegetables are popular once again.
Wearing facemasks is just for commuters now.
Mile-long queues at Tesco was last year's issue.
Just getting there has now usurped that pleasure.
Because, as summer turns to autumn, other concerns are at hand.
Long lines at closed petrol stations are the new thing.
For the legions of angry idiots to moan about.
It won't be for long; they'll be back on the road soon.
Driving around, searching for the next disaster du jour.

* * *

"SAY SOMETHING!!"

It was last Monday morning when I found my voice.

I sat down opposite the wife, about to eat breakfast.

Me, slumped over in my old dressing gown, her, pristine in an haute couture dress.

I realised that our personalities mirrored our breakfasts-

For me, porridge - lukewarm, grey and slightly lumpy.

For her, a grapefruit – sharp, clean and extremely sour.

And then, right on cue, it started.

'You know, you let people walk all over you.'

I ignored her.

'Talk to me. You should speak your mind.'

I stared at her blankly.

'Say what you mean, and mean what you say.'

I shrugged my shoulders.

'You always just sit there - vacuous and vacant.'

I nodded in concession.

Her whiny voice gave me a headache as it *always* did.

'Well, say something. Go on, surprise me.'

I thought for a moment, cleared my throat and took a deep breath.

'Well, your dress is hideous, your tone is obnoxious, and I slept with your sister.'

I sat back with a huge sense of relief. I'd done exactly what she asked.

So here I am, a week later, sitting at the same breakfast table.

I'm still wearing the same old dressing gown.

And I'm eating the same old lumpy porridge.

However, on the plus side, my headache has gone.

* * *

PRE-HOLIDAY PANIC

It's the day our holiday starts; we've been waiting quite a while.
Checking the list of things coming with us; many weeks to compile.
Apart from clothes and toiletries, there's so much stuff to pack,
Sunscreen, plug adapters and, of course, a box of Prozac.

Passports, camera, passports, tickets, passports, insurance, passports, money,
All this last-minute paranoid checking really isn't funny.
Finding room in the car boot, trying to fit in luggage for four,
Finally, we're ready; everything's done; I firmly shut the front door.

As soon as I sink my ample posterior into the driver's seat,
My mind starts to race, and my face turns as white as a sheet.
I'm beginning to doubt myself and wondering if I've done,
All the things I needed to do before our two weeks in the sun.

What if I've over-estimated the weights of the luggage and bags?
And did I manage to successfully tie on all of the little tags?
Should I get out, open the boot and check all the cases –
Or trust my mind; put it through its paces?

I've remembered to nail up the cat flap, not that it served a use.
As poor kitty has long since scarpered, preferring a life on the loose.
The garage is "locked" with an old padlock, too rusty to close,
Not that there's much to nick in there– a Flymo and a garden hose.

All the TVs in all the rooms were definitely unplugged from the walls.
And not forgetting the Sky box, too. Phew! That was a close call.
The breadmaker is also powerless; I've alleviated all my fears.
Hang on; the breadmaker is in the loft, as it has been for many years.

The neighbours have been asked to put our bins out on the drive,
On Tuesday after 6 pm, the night before the binmen arrive.
That sort of genius will deter thieves, and will certainly rule out,
The threat of any potential burglary, of that, I have no doubt.

If that doesn't fool them, their dastardly progress surely will be
blocked,
By the secure windows and solid front door, which I *think* have been
locked.
Besides, the alarm will deafen them with a monotonous, high-pitched
shrill.
But, I'll choke on my Margarita if I get a call from the Old Bill.

Did I remember to call work and cancel the boss's meeting?
And switch off the hot water and turn down the heating?
Did I put away the PS4 in the cabinet next to the couch?
Yes, the wife saw me do that; at least, I think she could vouch.

So many things cross my mind before I get to the end of my road -
Was my laptop shut down, or was it left in 'sleep mode'?
I know I've checked the stove, and the knobs were in the 'off' position,
But is there a slight chance they could leak a gaseous emission?

What about the video recorder? Haha, no need to worry about that.
That's been gone longer than the breadmaker and the runaway cat.
Let me just check my pockets, for my wallet and my phone.
Yep, they're both present and correct. *Now*, I'm in the zone.

'Haven't you forgotten something?' my son questions his Dad.
'I don't think so,' I tell him. He thinks I've gone mad.
Then he points to the seat beside me—my wife isn't there.
So, I turn the car around, shout, 'Bloody hell!' and mouth a short
prayer.

Outside the house, she's standing, with arms folded tight.
'Did you like my little joke, dear?' Her stare fills me with fright.
'Just don't…' she sneers as she gets in; my "joke" has fallen well short.
It's going to be an uncomfortable drive to London Heathrow airport.

Oh, I've just realised the unplugged Sky box won't be able to record,
All the missus' programmes, which now won't be stored.
It's best I don't tell her until we're at least halfway around,
The M25 in two weeks' time, when we're driving homeward bound.

* * *

NOT QUITE OCD

I'm not quite OCD; at least, I don't think I am.
Just a few moments I'll take to wash my hands, then dry.
And the taps I'll turn them on and off only once,
With no concerns that anything will go awry.

I'll switch on the lights when I enter a room,
And then off again when I leave.
I've never felt the urge to repeat the task,
That's something I can't even conceive.

There are those who, when locking a car,
Press the button on the key a dozen times or more.
I just don't understand what goes through their mind,
For me, five or six is sufficient as an encore.

What about those who can't leave their house,
Without thinking they'd forgot to lock the front door?
They'll repeat the lock/unlock process for a full ten minutes,
Poor folks. At least I only do it for three or four.

* * *

FIRST DAY BACK

Preparing for the first day back at school,
It is quite stressful, and that's putting it mild.
The panic and the manic running around,
And I'm referring to the mother, not the child.

As her son pokes and paws at his cereal,
Whilst watching Sky Sports News on TV,
Mother is frantically trying to find,
His shorts and socks that he needs for PE.

'Are you sure you've got all your books?'
Mum asks her disinterested son in despair,
'I've already told you, they're in my bag,'
He mumbles back along with a defiant stare.

And what about your lanyard and identity card?
Without ID, they won't let you in school.
Her son casually opens up his blazer,
And coolly shows mum that he's no fool.

The daughter eventually sashays downstairs,
Layers of makeup plastered over her face.
'You can take that off, straight away,' bellows Mum.
And the girl storms off back upstairs in haste.

A few minutes later, her daughter reappears,
With a complexion as fresh as a spring morn.
'I want you home, straight after school, today.'
The girl, makeup-free but now full of scorn.

'But Mum, I'm in year ten now. I'm not a little girl.'
Moans the young lady, protesting her case.
Her brother, two years her junior, sniggers to himself,
And points at his sister, making a rude face.

'I don't know why *you're* so pleased with yourself,
You have a dental appointment at half four.
And don't expect it to be a short visit either,
Judging by all the sweet wrappers I found in your drawer.'

With breakfast over, the kids are ready,
Mum goes through her checklist once again -
'Books, pens, PE kits, Oyster cards...?'
Her children nod politely to appease old mother hen.

With a final inspection and straightening of ties,
Mum kisses and dismisses her brood without delay.
She opens the front door and waves them off,
No one has realised it's actually an Inset day.

* * *

I'M SCAMMING YOU

Hello. I'm a scammer, and I want your money.
Although I'll pretend I'm really a nice guy.
I want to confirm all your bank details with you,
If that's not too much to ask before I say goodbye.

You've probably received one of those awful emails,
From someone purporting to be a Nigerian Prince,
Saying that he wants to deposit lots of money,
Into your bank account, which later, he'll rinse.

That's just so impersonal, don't you think?
What I'm doing is far more polite and direct.
I don't even know your name yet, Mrs... ah, Taylor.
I'll rob you blind, but with due care and respect.

Do you have your bank details to hand Mrs Taylor?
What's that? Oh, Sylvia. You can call me Billy.
That's not my real name, of course. Oh no.
I won't give you that. I'm not totally silly.

What's this for? Let's say I'm updating our security.
I'm from the bank, and I'm making sure your account is fine.
Does that sound genuine and authentic to you, Sylvia?
Good. I *thought* that was a pretty good line.

OK. If you could start with your account number.
Sorry, was that last digit a nine or a five?
We want to be as accurate as we can, don't we, Sylvia?
Before I add your details to my personal archive.

Right then, that's your bank details taken care of.
I see it's your birthday next week?
Oh, it was last month on the 29th. You were 75?
Well, belated happy birthday... (you decrepit antique).

Thank you for being so accommodating, Sylvia,
It was a pleasure, but now we are through.
What's that? You closed this account six years ago?
You've been leading me on? Well, fuck you!!

* * *

A HAND-WRITTEN PLEASURE

Handwritten birthday cards, I remember them well.
It's what I used to discard as soon as I opened a present.
Of course, that's when I was just a kid,
Nowadays, to receive one really is most pleasant.

The ease of sending a greeting on social media,
Has relieved many of us of the need,
To match the picture and sentiment of a card,
In an real shop, by way of a good deed.

We don't even have to remember the date,
As Facebook reminds us on our profile page.
That our nearest, dearest and those we hardly know,
Will be adding another year to their age.

Of course, there are online applications we can use,
To create and deliver a card to those who deserve.
A personal greeting and even a gift of some description,
But in most cases, our time and money we'd prefer to conserve.

Now the kids are more mature, so they've moved on,
From making cards at school to buying them in a shop.
It won't be too long before *I* get the Facebook greeting,
Or perhaps a 10-second Tiktok made on the hop.

I'm at an age now where presents don't mean much;
It's the thought that goes into writing a card I cherish.
Whether it be from a family member or close and dear friend,
Even if the sentiment is tacky and the picture garish.

* * *

CHARGING CABLES

'There has to be one that works somewhere,'
Is the thought going through my head,
During the ongoing search for a charging cable,
For my phone, that's battery is dead.

The red one, the blue one, the grey one too,
None of them work efficiently, if at all.
And the tangled, insulated striped cable,
Only charges my phone at a crawl.

The short white one with exposed wires,
The long one with a wobbly USB connection,
I hang on to all my redundant lengths of cord,
Adding them to my useless cable collection.

I do have one that just about works,
If I wrap it around my phone very tightly.
And one that's effective only if I smile,
For it to charge, I have to ask most politely.

I tend to buy one or two every month,
From online retailers, quite extensive.
They're not all cheap or economy brands, though.
Normally, they're 'top quality' and expensive.

The ones that do seem to work most regularly,
Unfortunately magically disappear.
From the lounge to the childrens' bedrooms,
Although how they get there is never made clear.

The only cable that works, I assume,
Is the green one that's wound up on the bookshelf.
It has USB-C connection that nobody uses,
How did it get there? No one knows, least myself.

I would honestly pay a princely sum,
For a cable that will effectively charge,
And remain in one place, and never escaping.
So, my useless collection, I won't need to enlarge.

* * *

DE-LEARNING TO DRIVE

'Teach me to drive, Dad,' my teenage daughter appealed.
'But I'm no driving instructor,' I sadly revealed.
I've driven automatics for thirty-odd years,
I couldn't imagine using a clutch with five forward gears.

My own driving lessons are just a faint blur,
I've learnt some terrible habits, everyone would concur.
'Ask your mother; she's more patient than me.
And *her* licence is clean; completely point-free.'

'Mirror, signal, manoeuvre', my instructor told me to do.
Now I just manoeuvre; sod the other two.
'Hands at ten to two on the steering wheel,' he said.
I keep one hand at half-past; the other props up my head.

And as for stopping distances, what are they supposed to be?
A hundred metres doing 50–or was it thirty-three?
Oh, and the emergency stop, so to avoid a crash,
I still practice them when the speed cameras flash.

There was something about keeping your eyes on the road,
And, of course, the signs from the Highway Code.
I can no longer remember what they all warn,
Though, I'm sure there was one meaning, "Keep off the lawn."

Do I always indicate? Oh, don't be a dreamer,
I'm exempt by law because I drive a Beamer.
Reversing around corners and performing three-point turns;
I use my own patented methods; have no concerns.

The modern theory test, I could never have passed,
Answering 50 questions, it's quite a contrast,
To *my* test, when I was shown a picture on the day,
And all I had to recognise was the sign for 'Give Way'.

You may think I'm careless; a bit of a tool,
But I'm totally aware, till I run out of fuel.
And I usually buckle-up, because I want to survive,
The many idiots on the road who think they can drive.

* * *

A PERFECT POEM?

My speeling might sometimes be por.
My grammar could maybe is bad.
My punctuation! Is sometimes: slightly off-kilter"
And I Put capitals in All the wrong plaCEs, which is woRse.
I might use apostrophe's in plural's when I shouldn't.
And go for an extra line or two in a verse.

And not every line will chime with rhyme,
Not all the time, but that's no crime.
Some of my sentences might be a little too wordy and unnecessarily
long and then tail off as if I've lost my drift altogether and then…
Some are short.

My use of idioms may not ring any bells.
My use of alliteration won't hit the highest heights of (h)English that
you've heard.
My use of onomatopoeia may not sizzle like a well-oiled clock.
And from our American neighbors, I might borrow an oddly spelt
word.

I might be confused my tenses like I will do in my past.
But if your expecting me to fall into the trap,
Of not using the right words in they're right places,
Then I'm sorry, but I just don't give a crap.

I'm lucky I don't knead my autocorevetv very mush.
And I may be a little too fond of the literary cliche,
But at the end of the day, worse things happen at sea.
Like forgetting the last line of a stanza - okay?

I might not of realised that it's "have" and not "of",
Until it's far too late to correct it to a tee.
And I may accidentally repeat an earlier line,
But at the end of the day, worse things happen at sea.

I might fall foul of using a double negative,
Even though it just won't do me no good in my view.
And finish the odd sentence with a preposition,
Which is a terrible felony, or at least it used to.

My use of hyperbole is a million times less than it was.
My fondness of idioms tends to go by the book.
The currency of my puns are in mint condition.
If you don't believe me, take a quick look.

But my imagination is still fluid to write a fine poem,
Even though my concentration sometimes wanes.
Before I finish a piece, I tend to pause and...

* * *

About the Author

This is Elliot Stanton's sixth book and his first book of poetry. Four of his previous books have been humorous novels, featuring aspects of real-life events. However, in the spring of 2019, he started writing a series of Tales of the Unexpected–type stories and 12 months later, there were enough to create *The Crimson Scarf and Other Short Stories*. During the pandemic lockdown in early 2021, Elliot started writing short poems on the things he'd seen and experienced. The culmination of his endeavours is this collection, *It Can't Be Just Me - Poetic Observations on Modern Life*.

His interests include history, watching sport, music and travel. His favourite location is Las Vegas, where he has visited many times. In fact, Vegas is the location of his second novel, *For A Few Dollars Less*.

If you've enjoyed reading this book, please leave him a review on Amazon. https://www.amazon.co.uk/review/create-review?&asin =B09K1XFR45

You can connect with me on:

- https://www.elliotstanton.com
- https://twitter.com/elboy44
- https://www.facebook.com/groups/1561342593910186

Also by Elliot Stanton

Available on Amazon as paperback and download or visit Elliot's website at https://www.elliotstanton.com

The Crimson Scarf and Other Stories
A collection of 17 short stories that will satisfy the imaginations of those who enjoy fiction with entertaining and unexpected twists.

In life, you don't always get a "happy ever after", no matter how hard you wish. Not every mystery can be solved, and occasionally the bad guy wins. While Karma dictates that wrongdoers get their comeuppance, and "what goes around, comes around", this is not always the case. Occasionally, what comes around has been around and gone elsewhere.

Some people are good: others do things for the right reason, but end up doing more bad than good; some set out to harm, but finally find a conscience and a few are evil through and through. The characters within *The Crimson Scarf and Other Stories* are diverse, and for many of them, the consequences of their actions do not always acknowledge the rules of Karma.

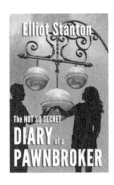

The Not So Secret Diary of a Pawnbroker

Middle-aged, married man with three grown-up children, Pete Dawson, an East London pawnbroker, finds himself living a predictable and quite often, boring life. Over time, an opportunity for change arises when his young, female work colleague takes an interest in him. it is a feeling which becomes mutual.

However, Pete starts to realise that something is not quite as it should be...

For A Few Dollars Less

A stag trip to Las Vegas doesn't go quite to plan. A nightclub fracas, a street altercation featuring film and TV "stars" is just the beginning. When things escalate to arms smuggling, a suspected homicide and a Mafia double-crossing, the members of The Syndicate soon realise that their vacation to Sin City was not what any of them expected.

Questionable Friends

They say it's not *what* you know, it's *who* you know. But, what happens when you find out that you don't know these people as well as you thought?

The journey from the sticky beer-stained tables of their local pub, to the slick, pristine studio set of a nationwide television quiz programme is swift. However, for Mike Knight and his team of quizzers, events unfold that change all of their lives.

To coin a phrase - Keep your friends close, and your fellow quiz teammates even closer.

The Not So Secret Diary of a Store Detective

Five years have passed since the events of *The Not So Secret Diary of a Pawnbroker* and recently divorced Pete Dawson begins work as a supermarket store detective. Matters outside his control continue to concern him; none greater than the actions of the incumbent U.S. President and the closure of his local Chinese takeaway. However a chance meeting with an enticing ghost from his past gives him much to ponder.

The Not So Secret Diary of a Store Detective is an amusing and entertaining insight into the life of a worried man whose mid-life crisis is happening right before his very eyes.

Printed in Great Britain
by Amazon

81498292R00078